This book belongs to

Passionate Ninja

A Book About Finding What Makes Your Heart Dance With Joy

Ninja Life Hacks®
by Mary Nhin

L is for **Listen**. My journey began when I decided to listen carefully to all the things around me. I listened to the birds chirping, the wind whispering, and even the giggles of children playing. I realized that paying attention made everything more exciting!

O is for **Observe**. Next, I learned to observe. I watched the ants work hard, the flowers bloom, and the stars twinkle at night. There was so much beauty in the world when I took the time to look closely.

V is for **Value**. As I observed, I started to value every little thing that made me happy. My favorite book, my playful puppy, and even the warm hugs from my family. These were the treasures that made my heart feel full.

E is for **Explore**. With my newfound appreciation, I went on an adventure! I tried painting, dancing, and even gardening. Each new activity brought a new spark of excitement into my life.

After the performance, many ninjas approached us, telling us how our songs and drawings made them feel so happy. It was the best feeling in the world to know that our passions brought joy to others.

So never stop **listening** to your heart. **Observe** the beauty around you, **value** the things that make you happy, and **explore** what brings you joy. Who knows, you might just discover your own special passion too!

Remembering, L.O.V.E. could be your secret weapon in finding what makes your heart dance with joy. And when you find it, share it with the world, and watch how your passion grows!

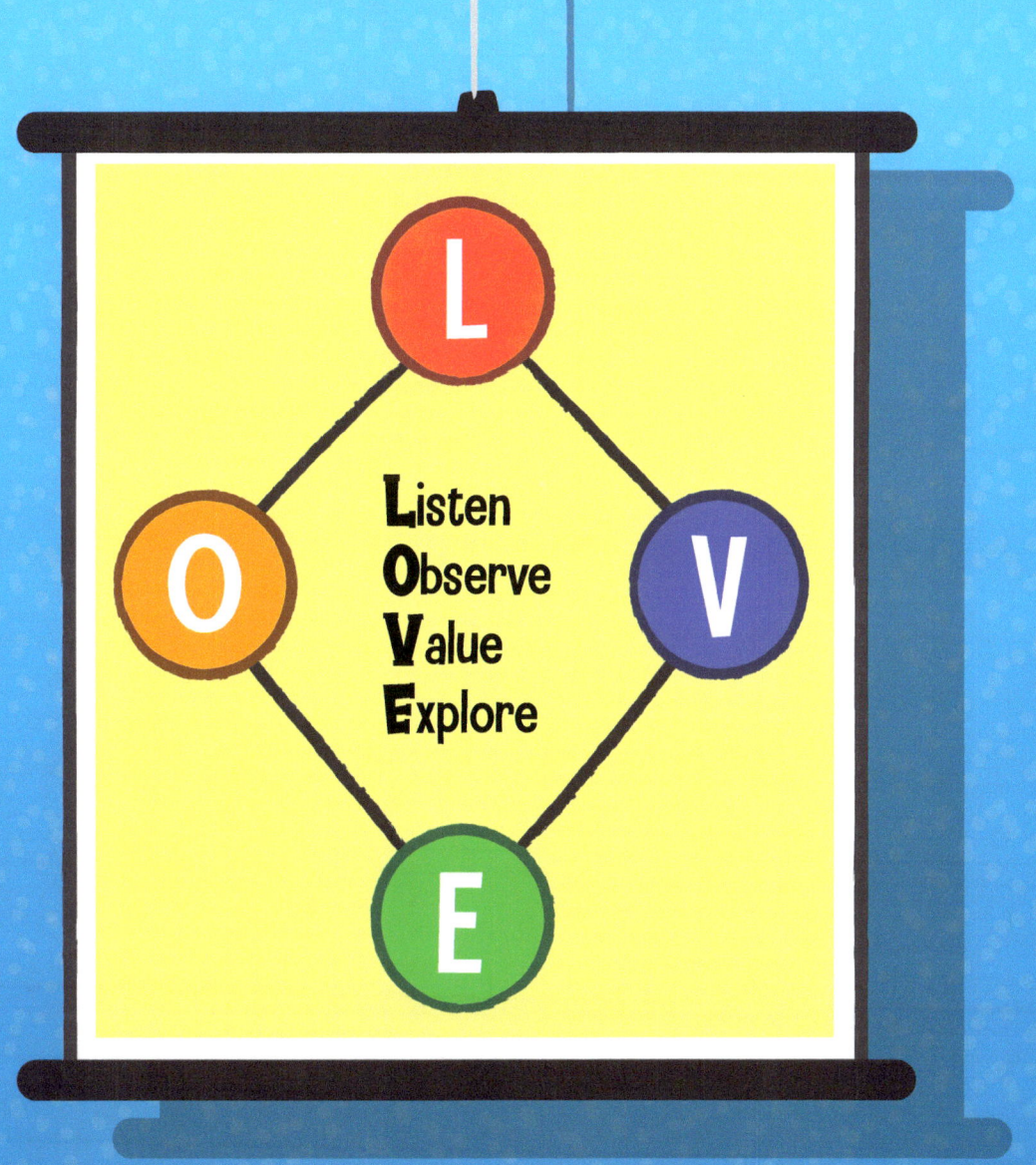

Continue the learning with the Passionate Ninja lesson plans which include superpower skills practice, STEM activity, craft, and more!

Instagram: @marynhin @officialninjalifehacks
#NinjaLifeHacks

YouTube: Ninja Life Hacks

Facebook: Mary Nhin Ninja Life Hacks

TikTok: @officialninjalifehacks

www.ingramcontent.com/pod-product-compliance
Lightning Source LLC
Chambersburg PA
CBHW041522070526

44585CB00002B/43